Produced by Kroha Associates, Inc.
Middletown, Connecticut

Printed in the United States of America.

ISBN 1-56326-161-8

Castles In The Sand

"It's so beautiful!" said Sandy the fish.

"A real work of art," agreed Sebastian the crab.

They were talking about the sand castle Ariel had been building all morning. It had six towers and twelve windows, and there were two sea horses standing guard at the gate.

"Do you really like it?" the Little Mermaid asked shyly.

"Like it? I love it!" Sebastian said, examining the drawbridge.

"Be careful!" Ariel cried out. "It's very fragile."

Just then they heard Scuttle calling out to them. "Gangway! Look out below!" he cried. The eager seagull was coming in for a landing, and he was headed right for Ariel's sand castle!

"Scuttle! Watch out!" shouted Sebastian.

"Be careful! You're going to crash!" cried Sandy.

But it was too late.
Scuttle skidded across the
sand, did two somersaults,
bounced up into the air —
and landed beak-first, right
in the middle of Ariel's sand castle!

"Hey, who put a sand castle on
my landing strip?" sputtered Scuttle.

"What do you mean *your* landing strip?"
Ariel cried. "I've never seen you land here before. Now
look at what you've done to *my* sand castle! It's ruined!"

"It's not ruined!" the bird replied. "I can fix it!"

Scuttle carefully picked up one of
the broken towers, but as he did his tail
smashed into the castle and brought it crumbling down.

"Oh, Scuttle, you've made things worse!" Ariel moaned.

"But I barely touched it!" protested Scuttle.

"Ariel," said Sebastian, "Scuttle didn't mean to ruin your sand castle.
It was an accident." But Ariel didn't hear him — she was already
swimming away.

Ariel didn't stop swimming until she reached Scales's cave.

"You should have seen him!" she said to the dragon. "He landed on my sand castle on purpose!"

"That doesn't sound like Scuttle to me," said Scales. "He may be a little goofy sometimes, but he wouldn't deliberately aim for your castle."

"He did it on purpose all right," Ariel fumed. "This whole thing is his fault!"

But Scuttle had other ideas. "It's Ariel's own fault her castle got ruined,"
he complained to Flounder later that day. "She knows that's where I always
land. And besides, how sturdy can a castle be when it's made out of sand? A
good strong breeze could have knocked that castle over."

The next day, Ariel and Scuttle were still angry with each other. Scales tried to make things better by inviting them both to breakfast, but Ariel refused to eat with Scuttle. "I might accidentally put my plate where Scuttle wants to sit," she snapped.

Flounder and Sandy thought a game of ringtoss would do the trick, but Scuttle didn't want to play because Ariel was there. "I might accidentally stand where she wants to throw," he said.

"It's no use," sighed Scales. "We'll never get them to apologize to each other."

"Let's go see Sebastian," said Sandy. "I bet he'll know how to handle this."

"What we have to do," said Sebastian, "is get them to understand each other's feelings."

"But how?" Scales asked.

"We can't even get them to speak to each other," added Sandy.

Sebastian thought for a moment. "Scales, you tell Ariel that Scuttle wants to apologize. Flounder, you tell Scuttle that Ariel wants to apologize. I'll take care of the rest," he said, pleased with his clever plan.

Later, Ariel and Scuttle met Sebastian by the lagoon.

"Okay, apologize," Ariel said to Scuttle.

"I thought *you* were going to apologize!" the startled bird replied. "Sebastian, you tricked us!"

"As long as we're here," Sebastian said, "let's play a little game. Scuttle, you pretend you're Ariel, and Ariel, you pretend you're Scuttle. That way you'll each see how the other one feels."

"That's silly," Scuttle said. "She can't fly!"

"And seagulls are not at all like mermaids!" said Ariel.

"Please," Sebastian pleaded, "give it a try."

"Okay," said Scuttle grudgingly. Then, perched on the rock pretending to be Ariel, he said in a high, squeaky voice, "Scuttle, you clumsy bird, I worked hard making my castle and you landed on it! Now *you're* upset." Suddenly Scuttle stopped. He was beginning to see how Ariel felt.

Next Ariel flapped her arms and pretended to be Scuttle. "Here I am landing on the beach. What's that below? Uh-oh. Ariel's sand castle is right where I want to land. Now *she's* angry with me." Then Ariel was quiet. She was beginning to understand Scuttle's problem, too.

Sebastian's plan was working. "You see?" he said. "Friends need to understand each other's feelings."

Later, Scuttle started feeling sorry about the way he had acted. "Ariel's my friend," he told Flounder. "I didn't mean to wreck her sand castle. But that's my favorite place to land. Now I don't know what to do."

Ariel didn't know what to do either. "I'm sorry I built my sand castle on Scuttle's favorite landing spot," she told Scales. "But there's no other place for me to build my sand castles, and he can land anywhere he wants to! Still, he's such a good friend. I wish we weren't fighting like this."

The next day, Ariel went to the lagoon to be alone and think. But Scuttle was already there. "I don't like being angry with you," he said softly. "I'm sorry I ruined your castle. But that sand crumbles so easily."

"And I don't like being angry with you, either," said Ariel. "I'm sorry I built my castle where you like to land. But there's nowhere else for me to build things."

"I guess I could find someplace else to land," said Scuttle.

"And I guess I could make my castles out of clay instead of sand. Then they'd last longer," Ariel replied. "But I'm a mermaid. How am I supposed to get clay from a faraway valley?"

"That's easy!" replied Scuttle. "I could get it for you!"

"That would be great!" Ariel replied. "And I could make a special landing strip on the beach for you to use whenever you want!"

While Scuttle was off getting the clay, Ariel got Scales to help her build the landing strip out of seaweed and palm fronds. "Wow, this is the best landing strip I've ever seen!" Scuttle called out as he came back with Ariel's clay.

"I have another surprise for you, too," Ariel said mysteriously.

"I think my first new sculpture should be of you, Scuttle," Ariel said. "For helping me get the clay I need to make sturdy castles." As she put the finishing touches on the statue, Sebastian and Scales came by.

"Well, look at that!" cried Sebastian. "I guess you two are friends again, hmm?"

"It's a lot more fun than being angry," Ariel explained to Sebastian.

"Friends just need to understand each other's feelings," added Scuttle.

"You don't say!" said Sebastian. "Now, why didn't I think of that?"